First American Edition published in 2009 by
Enchanted Lion Books
201 Richards Street, Studio 4,
Brooklyn, NY 11231

Originally published in Denmark as *Højt at flyve* by Carlsen
Text and illustrations © 2002 by Jørgen Stamp
Translation © 2009 Enchanted Lion Books

Editorial Director: Birgitte Theilst
Design and layout: Mogens Christensen

[A CIP record is on file with the Library of Congress]

ISBN 978-1-59270-089-9

Printed in China by South China Printing Co., Ltd.

Flying High

Jørgen Stamp

ENCHANTED LION BOOKS

NEW YORK

Like all normal giraffes Walter had a long neck with a head at its end. But even though his head towered high in the air, Walter wasn't quite content.

"Just think how amazing it would be if you could fly," Walter said to himself as he looked dreamily up at the clouds. "Just think how incredible it would be to zoom up and down in the air at a staggering speed, doing somersaults and racing the birds. Or how fantastic it would be to fly off and discover the world!"

From sheer excitement, Walter got that sinking feeling that occasionally comes on after a great burst of enthusiasm.

In an old book Walter found some diagrams showing how to build a real airplane.

The Big Book of Airplanes

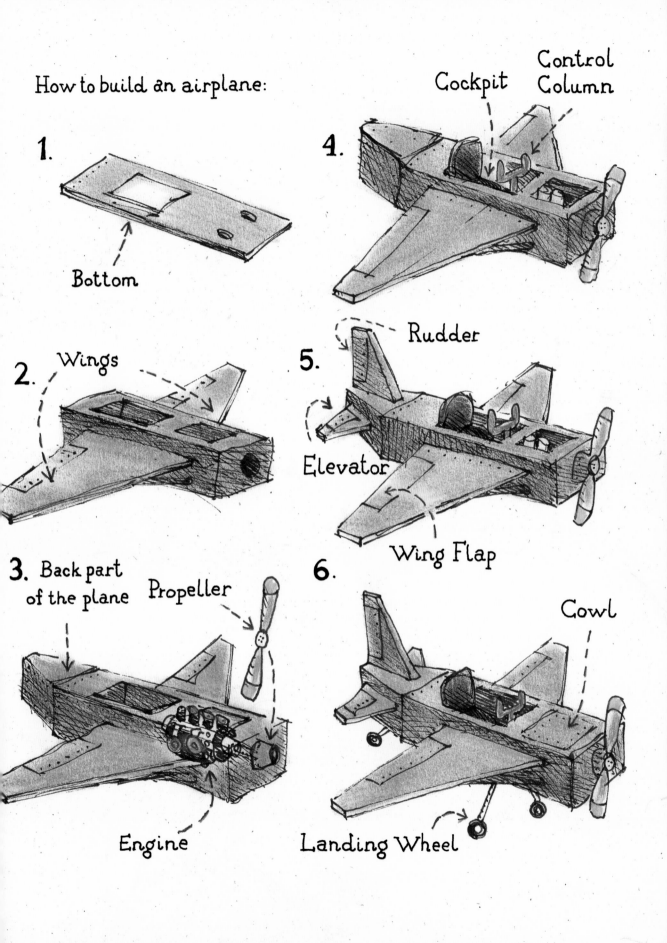

How to build an airplane:

1. Bottom

2. Wings

3. Back part of the plane — Propeller — Engine

4. Cockpit — Control Column

5. Rudder — Elevator — Wing Flap

6. Cowl — Landing Wheel

"I'll start right away," Walter shouted with joy and hurried off to get his toolbox and some wooden boards.

After Walter had worked for a while, Sonny the turtle came trudging by.

"Hello, Walter. What are you doing?"

"I'm building an airplane."

"Isn't that very difficult?" Sonny asked, his eyes wide with surprise.

"It certainly is!" said Walter importantly. "And please be careful. You could hurt yourself with all of these tools lying around." Walter looked very serious.

"Can I accompany you on a flight when you've finished your plane?" Sonny asked.

"I'm not sure there will be enough room," Walter replied. "Besides, I don't think turtles can stand flying as fast as my airplane will go."

"Oh," Sonny mumbled, feeling a little hurt.

"You see, it will fly a thousand times faster than you can go on a scooter," Walter said proudly.

"But I've never even tried a scooter," Sonny fretted.

"Well then!" said Walter. "In that case how could you be able to fly at all?"

"Oh… I guess not," said Sonny, feeling worse than ever as he trudged away.

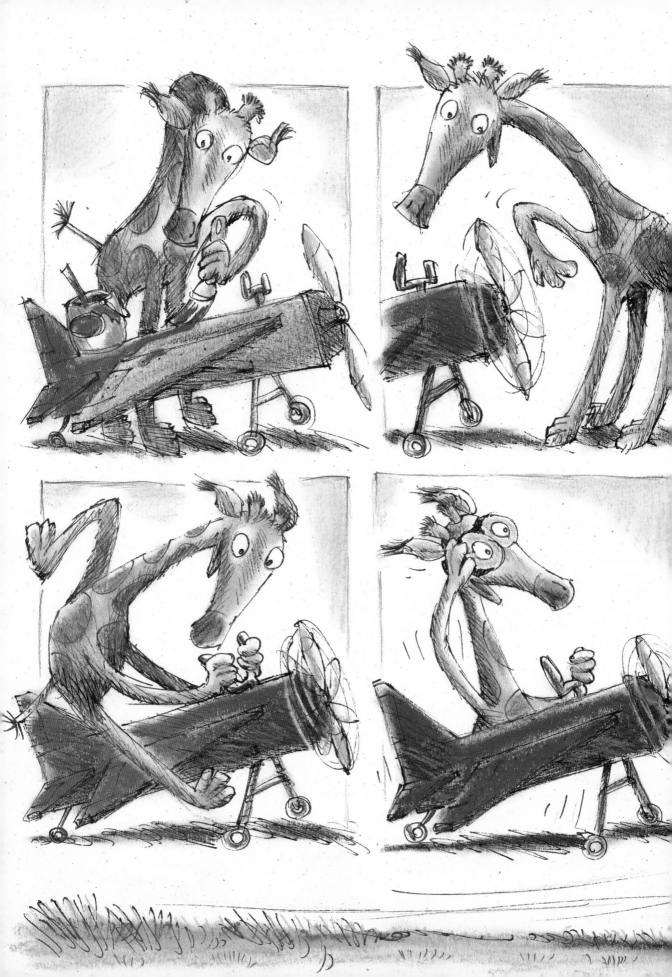

At last Walter finished his airplane.

"Time for take off," he cried eagerly and started up his engine.
The propeller began to turn, the engine increased in speed, and
Walter and his airplane took off!

"Hooray, I'm flying! Look at me, I'm
flying!" Walter shouted happily. "Hello,
little birds. Look at me. I'm flying!
Hello gull! Hello stork!"

Walter dived and looped. He turned
right and left. "Wheeeee!" he shouted at
the top of his lungs. "This is just like
going to the amusement park, only a lot
more fun!"

"Watch out!" a bird suddenly tweeted. "There's a storm coming."

"Ha! Ha!" Walter cried with pleasure. "I've got the best airplane in the world. It can put up with all kinds of weather."

A big flock of swans thought otherwise. "There's a storm ahead!" they called. "Hurry up and get away before it gets here." But no matter what anyone said, Walter didn't care.

"Just fly home you chickens!" he called. "I'm a world champion when it comes to flying. I'm not afraid of a few black clouds!"

But suddenly there were many big black rain clouds and lightning.

All at once a huge bolt of lightning hit the little airplane, tearing it in two. Walter's plane was going to crash.

"Oh no! I'm going a little too fast," he thought. Then he cried as loud as he possibly could, "He-e-e-elp, I'm falling! He-e-e-elp!"

Down by the lake Sonny was hiding from the storm under the trees. When he looked up at the sky to see if the storm would soon end, he was horrified to see Walter and his airplane crashing right into the lake.

Without hesitating, Sonny rushed into the water and swam as fast as he could. "Hold on, Walter!" he cried. "I'm coming!"

Kicking and splashing, Walter desperately tried to stay afloat in the middle of the lake. "I can't swim," he choked.

"Don't worry, I'll save you!" cried Sonny. "Climb up on my back!"

Walter struggled hard and finally made it onto Sonny's shell. Then, with Walter on his back, Sonny swam ashore.

All of the other animals were waiting there to help.

"That was amazing!" Walter panted as he sank down to the ground with exhaustion.

"Thank you so much, Sonny," Walter added a little shyly. "You are a really brave turtle, and a real friend…. Not like someone else I know," he went on, thinking mostly of himself.

The very next day Walter built a new airplane, and this time it had room enough for two!